It was a perfect Spring day. "Come on," said
Lily. "I want to go on a picnic and fly my kite.
Let's ask Mum."

Lily asked if Teddy could come and, of course,
he could. So they gathered up the picnic things
and the kites, and set off.

Ian Beck

Alone in the Woods

First published in 2001 by Scholastic Ltd
This edition first published in 2008 by Scholastic Children's Books
Euston House, 24 Eversholt Street
London NWI IDB
a division of Scholastic Ltd
www.scholastic.co.uk
London ~ New York ~ Toronto ~ Sydney ~ Auckland
Mexico City ~ New Delhi ~ Hong Kong

Text and illustrations copyright © 2001 Ian Beck

ISBN 978 1407 10807 0

Halfway up the steep hill, Lily asked, "Are we nearly there yet?"
"Not far," said Mum. "We'll be there soon."

At last they reached the top of Windy Hill.

They chose the perfect spot.

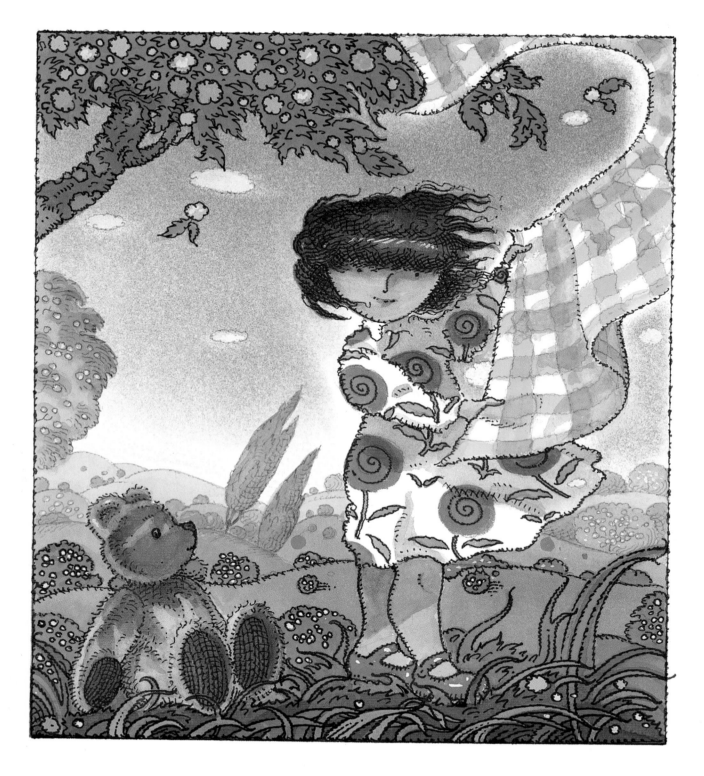

They laid out the cloth for the picnic.
Lily set Teddy down under a tree.

"Poor old Teddy," said Lily. "There's none for you, but you don't need a picnic, do you?"

After the picnic Mum said, "Let's fly
a kite. Which one shall we take?"
Lily chose the yellow one.

So Mum and Lily set off, leaving Teddy all alone to guard the picnic.

Suddenly a great gust of wind blew, and
tugged at the red kite. The kite lifted,
and, oh dear, tugged at Teddy.

Teddy bump, bump, bumped along the ground.

He was lifted over some prickly brambles and just missed a cowpat.

As the kite lifted higher and higher, Teddy was dragged through a hedge backwards.

He held on to the kite string with all his might because he was . . .

. . . flying! High up in the air. Now he was higher than the clouds.

He flew as high as an aeroplane.
"Whee!" waved Teddy.

Higher, higher and higher still, but this was fun!

Then suddenly the wind dropped, and the kite began to fall down through the clouds.

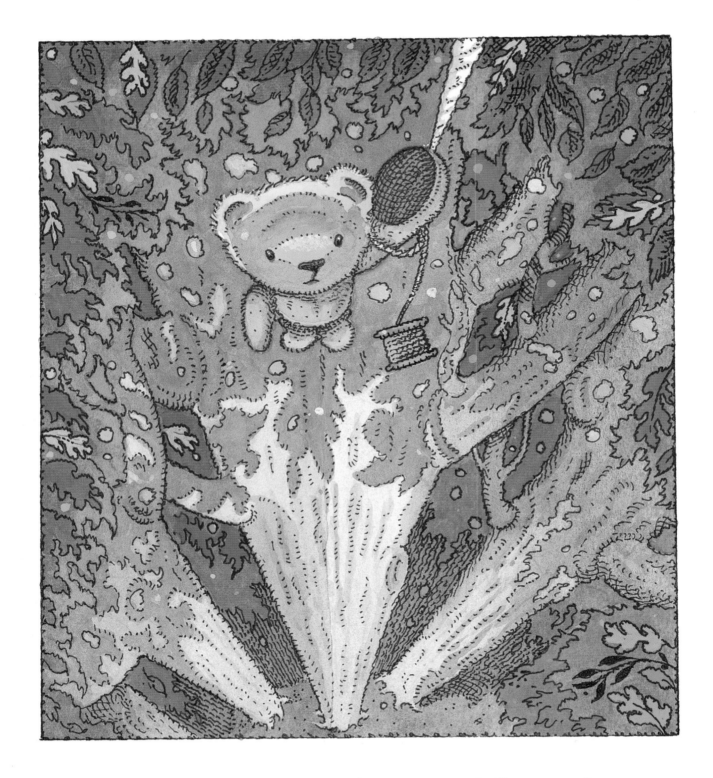

And Teddy fell with it, faster and faster, lower and lower, down, down into the woods until . . .

. . . he landed 'plop', into something green
and sticky! He heard voices whispering in
the bushes.

When he looked up Teddy saw bright
eyes looking at him. He felt frightened.
Teddy was alone in the woods.

Then slowly, out of the shadows they stepped,
first one, then two, three, four, and then more,
and more, and more, Teddy Bears.

"You landed in our best jelly," they said.
"Never mind, don't be shy, tuck in, it's a
party, it's a . . ."

. . . Teddy Bears' picnic."
They feasted on jelly and honey buns and
lemonade, and then they all had a little sleep.

When Teddy woke up, it was getting late.
"How will I get back?" he said.
"Don't worry," said the bears, "we'll help."

And so they did. It took a little while to get Teddy into the air, after all the jelly and honey buns.

But after one big heave, the wind lifted him,
above the trees, over the hills, and far away,
all the way back, until . . .

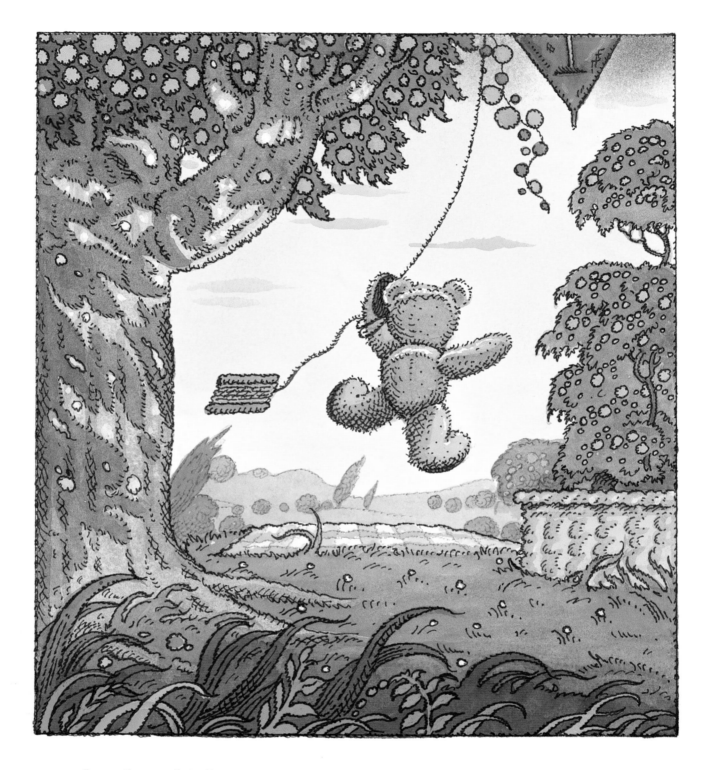

. . . he landed, very gently, with the softest bump, just where he had started.

When Lily and Mum came back, Lily said, "What a good Bear! You missed all the fun. Never mind. Come on, time to go home."

Good Night, Lily. Kiss kiss.
And Good Night, Teddy. Sleep tight.
But we know what really happened, don't we?